delight, almost a new invention after the long warm summer, the pub door wedge[illegible] open until eleven o'clock. There was a fir[illegible] grate, posters advertising the harv[illegible]nd a collecting bottle on the bar [illegible]es Christmas outing.

'Will you have a pi[illegible] know it's not agains[illegible]m the men by the [illegible] pint pulled almost [illegible] things being equal, I w[illegible]

They tired of th[illegible] we went to sit under the window by [illegible]ubber plant that always made me thin[illegible] the gourd which sheltered Jonah. Outside, on the corner, the lads with their motorbikes and the girls in their fluorescent anoraks laughed and chattered their way through a ritual older than any provided by the church.

'Let me tell you something. Seriously, Vicar,' said Michael.

'I might surprise you.'

'You going to confess your sins to the vicar, are you, Mike?'

'You'd be surprised as well, Stan Fox. I was devout once, you know.'

'What, only once?' said Stan with a chortle.

Michael's face took on a gaze of rare solemnity. 'My folks died when I was young, see. And I was brought up by the Sisters. Church every day. I was the altar boy for Father O'Malley. A chain smoker, Father O'Malley. He'd leave a half-finished fag end in the sanctuary before Mass – then have it lit up again before the words of the blessing were out of his mouth. He was a good priest. Like a real father to me. Then they moved him away – the mission field, some foreign parts – and we got this new priest, Father Martin. He was a tyrant. If he thought you were up to something you shouldn't have been, he'd stare at you over the top of his thick glasses. Then he'd wiggle his bony finger and whisper, "Come to me boy!" He made the shivers run down your back. The Sisters were scared of him too. And he was, you know, really religious. You couldn't relax. He always wanted to know if you'd said your prayers and what you'd prayed for. Then he'd find something you'd missed out and you'd have to say them all over again – "as a penance", he said. I couldn't wait to grow up, leave that place and give up religion altogether. And at last I did.'

There was a silence. Even wry Stan Fox looked full of sympathy as he sucked on his hissing pipe.

''Course,' resumed Michael, 'I still believe in God. But not in religion, if you see what I mean. Church and everything – I've had enough of it. Reminds me too much of Father Martin. "Mad

Martin", we used to call him, me and the other boys.'

The ale in The Acorn is always smooth, with a rich flavour of hops. A lovely amber colour, full and strong. A wonderful lubrication for long confessions. There were further details to Michael's autobiography. Enough storm and stress to make half a dozen gothic novels. It was Stan who eventually interrupted the flow – to remind Michael it was his round.

When Michael came back with the tray bearing three fresh pints, Stan said, 'You know, I've been thinking, Michael. I wonder why it is religion and churches never remind you of that decent padre – what was his name, O'Malley?'

Michael had no answer for him. It seemed barely a minute before Molly rang for last orders and the towels were over the pumps like a veil over the chalice. The guys with their girls and beloved motorbikes had gone home and the street was quiet under the high, bright moon, which raced across the sky behind some thin clouds. The church stood out black on the hill. It might have been a mysterious castle in Michael's gothic autobiography. We went off in opposite directions. I heard a chuckle on the breeze from Stan and Michael as I said goodnight to the Methodist minister's wife who was out walking her dog.

Michael didn't turn up at the harvest festival, but he appeared in my study the week after Christmas with a most presentable lady aged about thirty-five. Balding Michael and the slim blonde held hands like teenagers. I recognized her as the woman who had, last summer, moved into the stone cottage on the hill behind Jackson's farm, the cottage rebuilt out of what used to be the old windmill. Miss Holroyd had a hairdresser's salon in Knaresborough. When she moved in, Farmer Jackson had remarked: 'Clippin' 'air must pay better 'n clippin' sheep. Cost a bob or two, yon cottage.'

'Jean and me's come to see you about getting married.' Michael blushed, squeezed her hand. She gave him an encouraging smile. They asked for an April wedding, Saturday in Easter week.

'It is possible for us to get married in the parish church, is it, Vicar? I mean with . . .'

'With you being a Roman Catholic? Well, let's see. Are you a Roman Catholic too, Miss Holroyd?'

She was taken aback. Doubt and apprehension all over her face. She looked at Michael reproachfully. Then with great deliberation she said, 'No. I am not a Roman Catholic, Mr Mullen.'

The interview was beset with difficulties and delicacies. I tried to ease the tension with cheerfulness and routine. 'Of course you can be married in the parish church. No problem. But it would be a good idea to go and see Father Kennedy at Holy Family and let him know what you intend.'

'We don't want to get married in the Catholic church, Vicar!' He spoke with some vehemence.

'Well . . . I mean . . . if you're quite sure . . . I'll get in touch with Father Kennedy as well. Don't want him to think the Church of England is poaching his congregation, you know.'

'Michael may be quite sure, Mr Mullen, but I'm not!'

Cleary's country complexion turned white. 'But Jean – you promised!'

'Oh yes, I promised I'd marry you, Michael Cleary – and perhaps I shall. But I'll marry you in your own church.'

'But this is my church, here in Marton . . . isn't it, Vicar?'

My mind flew back to last autumn's night in The Acorn. Michael shuffled in his chair. The poor decent lapsed RC blacksmith seemed to be drowning. I threw him a lifeline. 'Of course the parish church is your church, Michael. It belongs to everyone in the parish. The Church of England belongs to the people of England. But we don't burn papists at the stake any more, so if you were baptized and brought up a Catholic – and that's what you told me – then you could perhaps be married at Holy Family.'

'I've told you – we don't want to be married at Holy Family.' He scratched his bald patch in exasperation. Miss Holroyd, her face on fire beneath the immaculate blond hair, stood up as if she was about to make a speech. 'Speak up for yourself, Michael! If you were brought up a Catholic, that's your proper Church. I don't want to be married anywhere . . .'

'Improper?' I ventured, smiling as broadly as I could before her passion and Michael's discomfiture. When she reddened, what a woman of spirit was revealed!

'Sorry, Mr Mullen. I was going to say "else". I don't want to be married anywhere else. I've nothing against your church, and it's kind of you to see us. But – and he never told me! – if Michael was brought up a Catholic, that's where he belongs. If I marry him,' – for the first time she spoke as if there might be some kind of doubt about the issue – 'that's where I belong, too.'

Michael shuddered.

I told them to go away and have a long think about it. If I could be of help, if they wanted me to get in touch with Father Kennedy, and so on, etc. . . .

They left by the side door that leads into the

garden. Michael all flustered and found out, Miss Holroyd alert, ablaze. They turned through the gate and set off at a fast pace up the hill towards Windmill Cottage. I telephoned Father Kennedy but Kate Hogan, who kept house at the presbytery, answered to say how the fathers were out: one was doing his Tuesday Bingo call and the other was hearing confessions – but she couldn't say who was doing which.

A week later, Father Kennedy rang me, his civilized Irish accent bubbling with mirth. 'Sure, there's rejoicing among the angels in heaven when one sinner repents – is that not right, Peter? Cleary – your blacksmith – has returned to the fold. And brought a fair lady with him. Though all me instincts tells me 'twas the other way about. She's receiving instruction. And Cleary's coming to the early Mass. Well now, I thought I'd tell you, in case you should think the fella's got himself infected with the religious mania.' It was an ecumenical phone call of great deliciousness.

Miss Holroyd and the blacksmith were married at Holy Family on the Saturday in Easter week. It was a pretty wedding and a most convivial wedding breakfast. I know, because I found myself sitting next to Stan Fox at the table nearest the bar.

I am reminded of the ecumenical spirit every Sunday as I stroll across to church to prepare for the early Communion and see Mr and Mrs Cleary climbing into their Mini to drive to the eight o'clock Mass at Holy Family.

10

TWO WORDS FROM THE OTHER SIDE

When the Reverend Murdoch A. Spry was vicar of St James', Barton, the parochial ministry of the Church of England took on aspects of surrealism. As big as Og the King of Bashan, ungainly as one of the larger mammals, he lumbered about the parish doing good violently to all and sundry. His career of outrageous exploits would have filled a catalogue before he married the head-mistress of the church school and went to a parish near the East Coast. There was his Youth Club trip to the Blackpool illuminations, when he managed to return having left seven of the youngsters in the fun fair. Even when faced with a posse of angry and distraught parents, his grin did not slip nor his geniality abate: 'I'll go back myself and fetch them in Mr Greenwood's van.'

Greenwood the grocer must have excelled in works of supererogation to allow the accident-prone cleric to chase off into the October night in his firm's only means of transport. Actually, Murdoch did not arrive at the Blackpool police station until dawn. 'Sorry if I'm a bit late, but I went wrong at Giggleswick.' The sergeant didn't know whether to be relieved because help had at last arrived or to wonder if he had an impostor – even a kidnapper – on his hands.

Twice Murdoch made errors in the calling of banns and, had he not been amiably corrected by one of the old choirmen, wedding nights might have been full of even more surprises than usual for a couple of couples. Once he turned up at the right time and the right day of the week for the archdeacon's visitation: only it was the wrong month. It was the wrong church as well, so he found himself in the middle of a deanery Mother's Union service. Even in these days of equal opportunities and anti-sexist resolutions in Synod, churchwardens (i.e. those commanded to attend the visitation) are overwhelmingly drawn from the male sex. But it never occurred to Murdoch to wonder why he was the only man among all those ladies or even why the archdeacon himself had not turned up, until, having innocently asked the MU secretary if she had had her articles examined, he was abruptly certified of his precise whereabouts by the vicar of Ottershaw's mother.

The Reverend Spry was a good scholar, a Master of Arts (and of goodness knows what else!) of the University of Oxford, an expert on all the early heresies which afflicted the Church. 'I like to listen to Murdoch at the Literary and

Theological Society,' said my friend John Trentham, Vicar of Bewes. 'He makes everything so easy to follow for a bloke like me who doesn't know his Arius from his Origen.' If only Murdoch had been able to adapt his familiarity with the labyrinthine world of Pelagianism, Montanism and the rest to finding his way through the streets and lanes of his own parish, he would have been made Archbishop!

His sufferings and persecutions threatened to exceed even those listed by the apostle Paul: twice he locked himself in church; once in the nethermost hell of the boiler room; four times ran out of petrol while on parish business; countless appearances in the wrong colour of vestments; once miraculously escaping a thousand natural cuts when he walked through a new glass door in a shopfront in York. Amazingly, none of these adventures dimmed his amiability. Genial Murdoch was known as 'Smiler' to many of his parishioners who were themselves amused by his cheerful accidentalism.

That quirk in human nature which makes us laugh in the most inappropriate places! I was at a deanery service once when Murdoch was in charge of the proceedings. 'Good morning,' he began correctly and followed up with, 'Today is the eleventh Sunday after Trinity . . .' The exasperated dry wit of the vicar of Bewley whispered in my ear, 'Is it, heck!' Now Murdoch could have got away with his error: most people in a congregation don't worry too much about what after Trinity it might be. But Murdoch's big ears were not just for ornamental purposes. Quick as a monkey he lurched, beaming, across to Tom Stack of Bewley and enquired in a voice every bit as loud as that in which he had delivered his erroneous announcement to the people, 'Well, where are we up to then, Ted? I mean, Tom!' There followed a long, loud conversation until Murdoch was ascertained of what day it was. An extra-liturgical use for a surplice: you can use the sleeve to cover your face while you recover from the giggles. It was like Morning Prayer by Laurel and Hardy.

This bumbling scholar was no mere archivist, his mind rooted in the distant logic-chopping of early Christian heretics, while his body was free from the bonds of sense to wreak humorous havoc in the tangible world: he was a gifted pastor. It was as if the chaos of his bodily movements were divinely compensated by a spiritual equilibrium far beyond the aspirations of his brother clergy who might outwardly seem better balanced.

Mrs Patterson, who kept the confectioner's shop in Barton, lost her four-year-old son – run over by a tractor as he stepped out from behind an ice-cream van. Murdoch saved her from despair. Corinne Patterson had suffered much already in extremely grisly divorce proceedings: her husband had gone off to live in London with the eighteen-year-old daughter of one of Corinne's best friends. When Paul was killed, she seemed to lose her mind completely and there was talk of mental hospital. Murdoch persuaded the local GP that, against all appearances, Corinne would recover quickest at home. He arranged for a neighbour, Dorothy Richards, a gentle, sensitive woman who was sacristan at Barton church, to stay with Corinne at night. Murdoch himself seemed to spend all his waking hours in the bereaved household. 'It was a crucifixion that lasted five weeks,' he told me later as we came out of a chapter meeting in Bewley.

'And then when things seemed a bit better,' said Corinne, 'he'd come every Tuesday and Thursday afternoon and stay for an hour. I can't tell you what I owe to him: my sanity, my soul, everything. In those days just after Paul was killed, Mr Spry was . . . well, like I imagine Jesus would have been. I was numb most of the time. I can't explain it properly, but it was just as if I'd handed over everything to Mr Spry; as if he was doing the living for me. He knew exactly how I felt from minute to minute. I was sort of dead really, but he was alive. And that somehow meant I was still a bit alive. There was still hope.'

When there was real necessity, he knew his Tuesdays from his Thursdays well enough!

The loudest catastrophe which will be forever linked with the name of the Reverend Murdoch Althestan Spry was a macabre event of which he was entirely innocent. But such was his reputation that he could hardly have hoped to escape criticism for this disaster. There's no smoke without fire as they say – especially not in the municipal crematorium.

Murdoch set off in his red Mini to conduct the funeral of Harry Hastings who had died aged eighty-one. 'A dear husband, dad, grandad and great-grandad' said the largest wreath. Another said 'From all at The Packhorse and Mule'. As luck would have it, Murdoch arrived early, so he had time to do his pastoral visitation act on the men who operated the furnaces 'in the kitchen' as they were wont to say. Brothers they were, not twins but much alike; small, bony creatures, in their black cassocks they looked like undernourished blackbirds. They greeted Murdoch with twin smirks; 'How are you doing Mr Murdoch? When's you getting married then?' It was the time of his courtship with the village headmistress in Barton. He brushed their question aside. 'Tell me boys, did you get your pay rise?'

'Oh yes, sir. We've money to burn now!' As he said this, he pushed a button and a quiet whirring came from behind one of the furnaces. The other scrawny assistant called out, 'Come and look at the new calcium remains machine, Mr Murdoch!' (He pronounced the 'i' in calcium like the 'y' in dye.) 'See, it's like a spin dryer. You puts calcium remains in and shuts t'lid. Then them stone balls belt about like barmy till all's done into a fine powder.' He pulled down the lid and a ferocious din arose from the tall cylindrical machine. The assistant grinned at Murdoch, a grin of demonic triumph. Then the other assistant reappeared, grimacing and gesticulating above the noise. His mate stopped the hurtling stone balls so he could hear the other's message, which he had guessed anyhow: 'They're here!'

Derrington's hearse passed slowly through the main entrance and along the wooded drive. A glorious day, all cherry blossom and birdsong. The sunlight gleamed on the quiet and quality car as it pulled up outside the oak-panelled door of the chapel. Half a dozen saloon cars drew up just behind it. Frail old Enid Hastings all in black, with a black veil and a bunch of yellow flowers in her hands, stepped slowly out of the first car. Derrington smiled gently and took her hand. Murdoch was in his proper place with the prayer book opened at the proper page. The computerized music played a sugary introit and the people sat down. Murdoch conducted a very nice funeral. It went beautifully until the very end. In the crematorium, there is a quaint gothic mechanism – a partition in the wall behind the bier. It is more or less circular, and when the parson pushes the button on his lectern marked 'Blessing' at the end of the service, this partition slowly opens, the woodwork dividing into six pieces like petals falling from a flower. At the same time, the top part of the bier moves forward and slides gently into the gap in the wall. Finally a curtain closes behind the coffin and the effect is thus generated among the mourners that the dear departed has passed smoothly to his final resting place; whereas the assistants in the furnace room know that it is only his penultimate resting place – a trolley placed discreetly behind the partition in order to receive the coffin. A trolley *usually* placed there. Even *almost always* placed there . . . But not this time, alas!

There was something wrong with the moving part of the bier. So when Murdoch pressed the 'Blessing' button, instead of a slow, smooth movement of the coffin, it lurched forward with a loud metallic 'Chung!' The mourners raised their bowed heads in alarm, those from The Packhorse and Mule wondering whether old Harry were returning for 'last orders'. The coffin dived through the gaping partition and there followed an enormous crash from what I suppose we must refer to as the other side. The blue curtain closed with smooth dignity but the enormous crash was accompanied by the loud utterance from the room beyond of two strange words, the second of which was 'Hell'. Charlie Martin in the front pew looked up startled, thinking, no doubt, that he had just heard old Harry's first comment on the quality of the afterlife.

Murdoch remained calm as an iceberg. He came out from behind the lectern and stood at the front of the nave, from where he quietly asked the mourners to stay in their places for a moment. Then he nipped through the side door into the furnace room and returned in an instant to say softly, 'All is well. A rather bad fault in the air conditioning plant, that's all.'

Who can tell whether the mourners were convinced? But Murdoch had pulled off a master stroke. The right word at the right moment. Unquestionably. What does it say in the poem? 'If you can keep your head, when all about are losing theirs, you'll be a man . . .'

The Reverend Murdoch Athelstan Spry was a giant of a man.

11

A LOCAL DRAMA

The St Luke's Players number six: Emily Wright, Jack Hornshaw, Kate Sanderson, Molly Paton, Ted Davies and the Vicar. We also recruit a posse of non-union labour to help with the lights, stage managing, tickets, posters and all the other epi-phenomena of live theatre. Our first meeting of the year is usually towards the end of September – after the first frost. Last year, we met in the vicarage, surrounded by the whiff of paint and turpentine, step ladders and rolls of wallpaper. 'Bring them through into the dining room,' said Barbara, 'where there isn't quite so much upheaval.' There wasn't *quite* so much upheaval, only a light covering of our Tom's Lego bricks and the trappings of our home duplicating service: we had been running off the letters about our annual Gift Day.

'Sorry we're rather cluttered. If we're talking about drama tonight, maybe it had better be kitchen sink!'

Molly thought we should try a Shakespeare. All brain power and blue rinse was Molly. Blue eyes under the blue rinse darting here and there, defying anyone to say we weren't good enough to try something by old Bill. Jack, the milkman, was the first to pour cold water on her suggestion: 'There aren't enough of us, Molly.'

'*I*'ve thought of that.' (I thought she would have!) 'I can lay my hands on some boys from Knaresborough Grammar School. They have an excellent drama department there.'

How the boys would react to the sudden laying on of wiry Molly's enthusiastic hands was a matter for conjecture.

'Nay, Molly,' said Fred, as if cajoling one of his horses, 'let's do summat a bit simpler, like. I 'ad all on wi' your George Bernard Shaw, nivver mind your blank verse and all them murders.'

'We needn't do one of the tragedies, Mr Davies – or *murders* as you put it. We could try a comedy, *Twelfth Night* or *A Midsummer Night's Dream*.'

'It'd be a nightmare for me, old love!'

The old love fell silent.

'Well, I think . . .', Kate and Emily both spoke at once, then each of them stopped in deference to the other. Emily started again: '. . . we should do something modern for a change. Something like . . .'

She didn't get a chance to finish as Molly chirped up, 'Oh, quite, quite! Beckett, Pirandello, Ionesco, Pinter, Kurt Weil . . .' It was as if she were reading a Modernist telephone directory.

'What, all at once, Molly?', said I, fiddling with two bits of Lego.

'I meant J. B. Priestley, actually,' said Emily.

'*Time and the Conways* or *I Have Been Here Before*,' said Kate with much excitement.

Molly gave out what I can only describe as a refined snort. 'Priestley!' she exclaimed, screwing up her face, as if poor old J. B. were the harbinger of some dread disease. 'He's so preposterous, so embarrassing! All that philosophical stuff – and on the Yorkshire Moors of all places!'

'And what's matter wi' that?' asked Ted. 'Folks knows a thing or two in them 'ills,' – he flicked his thumb in the direction of Bailden – 'They in't simple.'

'Why don't we do another Gilbert and Sullivan then?' asked Jack, thinking he was introducing a spirit of compromise. There was a chorus of 'Not again!' just as Barbara walked in with the coffee. She must have thought they meant 'Not coffee again,' she looked so despised and rejected.

'We don't know what to do next,' I said.

'That makes two of us,' said Barbara. 'I've to speak to Mrs Duffield about changing the time of the choir practice *and* to see if Pauline Miner wants one of Alison Kettering's pups.'

'I didn't know young Alison 'ad 'ad pups!' said Ted, his round red face turning a deeper shade of purple. 'Pass the sugar, will you?'

Barbara said, 'Why don't you do what they did at the college the other year? You know, that thing with the court scene . . .'

'*Witness for the Prosecution*?' said Kate.

'Kafka?' said Molly.

'Neither,' said I. 'What a good idea! Yes that *would* go down well in Marton. I can see it now. 'Course, we'd need the help of Molly's boys from the school. But the church building would lend itself, it would be just right. Just the atmosphere we'd want.'

'In church?' said Emily, pulling a face as if she had burnt her lips on the hot coffee. 'Do you really think that the church is a suitable place for . . . a play?' I sensed the ghost of her Calvinist grandmother who had died the year before, killed in a coach accident between Lucerne and Geneva.

'Suitable for *this* play Emily? Certainly!'

They were patient as I told them about *The Verdict is Yours*, a play without a script. And I couldn't even remember its author's – or I should say its deviser's – name. 'The trial of Christ in an English courtroom. Or rather, the trial of his disciples. Take, say, six notable Christians from the New Testament and from any other period of church history, and have them examined and cross-examined by counsel.

Why do they believe? Aren't they just mistaken, deceived and so forth? The audience – the congregation if you like – are left to make up their own minds. *The Verdict is Yours*, see?'

'How d'you know what to say then, Peter, if there's no script?' Taciturn Jack and more cold water.

'That's just it. We invent the script as we go along in rehearsals. Suppose you're playing Counsel for the Prosecution, Jack. You've six prominent Christian witnesses to examine. Say you take, who? – OK, Simon Peter. You study his character from the New Testament. Then you pick on his weaknesses and frame three or four questions around them. Well, you'd certainly pick on the fact that he denied our Lord. And maybe you'd have a go at him for being a simple, uneducated man. Where does he pretend to get his religious understanding from . . .'

'Simple folk 'as a damn sight more religion in 'em than clever devils!' No one contradicted Ted.

'. . . And the same with all the characters in turn. Then at the end there's the final speeches – for and against – and . . . Was there a judge's summing up when you saw it, Barbara?'

'No, that's just the point. It's all left to the audience.' She stood up quickly. 'Pups!' she said and vanished.

Rehearsals were a revelation. Ted took the part of Simon Peter. He was so real you could almost smell the fish. Exactly the right combination of simplicity and power. Kate, tall and elegant, played Pilate's wife. The milkman was Thomas Cranmer. Emily had just the balance of austerity and warmth to make a convincing Mother Teresa. Hands were duly laid on two talented lads from the grammar school to play Counsel for the Prosecution and Counsel for the Defence. The prosecuting counsel was absolutely right – a thin, mobile boy with a grey complexion, short curly hair, irascible. I thought of Bernard Levin. Defence was a tower of strength – blond, six feet tall, broad, a kind face. They let me play Martin Luther. What a task! There I stood, pecked at by the cynical brilliance of the young prosecutor. It was hard not to feel scared stiff.

The play went on on Good Friday evening. It was a bright, cold day early in April, thin yellow clouds scudding before the north-west wind across a pale blue sky, the daffodils nodding optimistically by the churchyard wall. The church was full. On Maundy Thursday we had stripped the altar to Jack Hornshaw's solemn, booming reading of Psalm 22. The place looked bare, stark, penitential. Duffield was playing quietly, a selection from the St Matthew Passion. At eight o'clock, lights down and one bright spotlight was turned on the middle of the chancel step – upon a white robe and a crown of thorns, a silent representation of the Person who was the cause of all our attending. And *we* were judging *Him*!

The mellow organ music was replaced by a loud rendering of the opening of Ben Britten's 'Young Person's Guide to the Orchestra' and the procession led into the chancel. The counsel in their wigs and gowns. Tom Gaunt, our Churchwarden Emeritus as the usher with his staff. And the witnesses in period costume. It was so stirring. It would be difficult to sustain Luther's combative attitude, overcome as I was by the solemn splendour of the scene. But sure enough, Luther's hackles began to rise when the cocky, sardonic prosecutor put it to me '. . . that you did what you did for the sake of power, Martin Luther. It was a personal power struggle, is that not right? You capitalized on the forces of unrest and disquiet in order to make a name for yourself. "Here *I* stand", you said, isn't that right? *I, I, I,* the ego of Martin Luther – not, as you have insisted, the proclamation of Christ!'

I almost expected the crown of thorns to move of its own accord. I was relieved when the cheerful blond Defence arrived to give me a bit of encouragement.

Emily's Mother Teresa made the audience

catch their breath. She was so unfussy, so matter-of-fact. Workaday holiness. A calm but melodious voice, an advertisement for sincerity: 'We look after the destitute and the desperate. We have no will or strength of ourselves to do that day after day. We are weak, sir, but Christ is strong. He is the strength of our arms and the force of our wills. He it is who works in us and that is the truth, whether you believe it or not, sir!' For a moment, even the sardonic young advocate seemed to falter.

There was a memorable exchange between the Prosecution and Cranmer: 'There are rewards,' snarled the Counsel, curling his lip, 'for the humble followers of this . . .' he waved in arrogance towards the white robe and the crown, '. . . Galilean. You ended up as an Archbishop Thomas Cranmer, a Prince of the Church?'

'I ended up on a bonfire, sir!' Devastating.

After the Counsels' speeches and the recessional march behind Tom Gaunt, the packed church did its best with the lumps in its throats and sang all three verses of 'O Sacred Head' while the bright light remained on the crown of thorns, now lonely as Calvary in the middle of the chancel. Then the organ was silent as we all went home.

Holy Saturday at half past six in the evening, and I was in the church, sitting in the seventeenth-century choir by the altar in the Lady Chapel. Ladies of the parish had done their work and the place was a paradise of spring flowers. Easter Eve is always charged with an atmosphere of imminent, irresistible power. We wait for the great stone to move once more. I was waiting for anyone who might want to come and make their confession before the festival, or who might just want to come and talk for a few minutes. Ten to seven and in came Molly Paton, looking upset and worn out. She sat in a pew halfway towards the back of the nave, her face buried in her forearms, her breathing heavy, sad. I waited. After a few minutes, she came forward, forcing a smile on to her face. It was like a watery sun in February.

'Molly!' She had been weeping.

'Peter – I want you to listen to me.' She sat in the adjacent chair. Her umbrella fell to the floor and she ignored it. 'I've given in at last. I'm going to make my communion tomorrow for the first time since I was a girl. It's unbearable – I mean it's been unbearable all these years. The nothingness. The bleak blackness. Just nothing. I never felt anything. I couldn't believe. I was like that Prosecutor – impervious to grace because of some overpowering cynicism which possessed me, which I really thought *was* me. And I went through the motions of being a Christian, except that I never took communion – as you know. I couldn't bring myself to do that.

'And I turned to art. Salvation through aesthetics, you know. Shakespeare, the moderns – tragedy, alienation, loss. And music. Beautiful music. I listened often but it was as if it wasn't for me, as if it could never belong to me. The Sanctus from Mozart's C Minor Mass – it never filled me with joy, just a sense of being separated from joy. And people, churchpeople – I despised them in a way. Of course, I was always polite. I co-operated. Did I feel sorry for them, for their ignorance, their credulity – or did I envy them? Both.

'When I looked into the face of the young man who played the Prosecuting Counsel, I saw myself. Clever scepticism. A stoic resistance to – *what?* That's what I wondered through all the rehearsals. Then last night – that boy was so good – when he came at me with his fierce questions, I loved him, I pitied him. I wanted to save him from himself. I wanted to say, "Give! Give in! Give yourself! You're not in the cold! You are loved, you are accepted! Grace is all round."

'And of course, I was seeing myself, talking to myself – being able to love myself for the first time. Tim – the Prosecutor – well, it was all a *real* act with him. He's a convinced Christian.

Goes to St Giles. He talked to me about it once or twice. He, the Prosecutor, talked to me! Ironic, isn't it?

'I knew I could make a success of my part in the play – you know at the beginning when the others were worried about doing something that doesn't have a script. But I know the New Testament pretty well, Peter. I knew I could play a convincing Mary Magdalene. It was when the Prosecutor gave me one of his unbelieving smiles, despising me for being gullible, for being a woman: "Why did you go to the tomb early in the morning? Why did you bother to take spices, Mary? Didn't your – friend – once say: Let the dead bury the dead?" And that's when it all happened. I heard myself saying, "Because I loved him! Because I still love him! Because he is alive and he loves me!" I was crying.'

'You were very good.'

'I wasn't acting, Peter. I was more *me* than I'd ever been before. Suddenly I belonged. I belonged to all those other people in the church. I belonged with them, too. It sounds silly doesn't it – but I knew I loved them, that I do love them all. As if they and I had been waiting for something. What? The ice to melt. Life. Grace.'

There was no need for either of us to say another word.

A coincidence: Easter Day and it was Molly's

turn to read the Gospel. She read beautifully, as always: 'The first day of the week cometh Mary Magdalene early, when it was yet dark, unto the sepulchre, and seeth the stone taken away . . .'

I saw her, Molly, racing through the dawn mist, the stone taken away, the sepulchre open.

12

FOR ALL THE SAINTS

Even a country parson is obliged to venture occasionally into the big city. We needed a new fridge. Actually, I loved the old one: it was huge, cream coloured, the same model as you will have seen on a hundred old black and white films in which it is always referred to as 'the icebox'.

'We must get rid of that old contraption,' said Barbara after she had banged her knee against it one breakfast time. At that moment the lovely old art deco icebox switched itself on with a great whirr and a judder.

'See,' I said. 'It knows you're talking about it!'

'It's too big,' she said. 'I've no room to move in here. And the freezer compartment is broken.'

So we went one Thursday, 'traipsing' (as my grandmother used to say) all over Leeds to find a new icebox. The city was hot, congested with cars, their bonnets and windscreens reflecting the bright sunlight among the tall buildings. A range of constructional styles sufficient to fill an architectural glossary. The nineteenth-century post office, black as the statue of the Black Prince in City Square. The old Majestic cinema – now a restaurant – like a piece of seaside baroque. And, behind the Queen's Hotel, the new station building loomed, oblong, gigantic – just like our old fridge in the back kitchen.

The man said we wanted an automatic defroster. Odd words in that urban heatwave. I, on the other hand, wanted a cold beer and a breath of fresh air. The shop was littered with harassed folk bending to examine a variety of household gadgets. They looked as if they were doing obeisance. I dreamed up the words of an unlikely hymn:

> 'God made you,
> God made me;
> Who made new technology?'

I was suddenly aware that Barbara and the cheerful assistant were waiting on me for some sort of answer. 'Pardon?' I said. The assistant, his mouth half open, his head cocked on one side, seemed to be hanging on my every word. I remember thinking we could do with a few more in church like that at sermon time.

'Or,' he said, prompting me, 'there's the double freezer with the adjustable shelf. Very handy that. One does accumulate bottles of such odd sizes.'

He looked so urgent, that salesman, so rapt. I

felt embarrassed that I hadn't really been listening. 'Yes, odd bottles,' I said, trying to sound as if I'd got bottles on the brain. 'We'll have that one then, please.'

He performed a lightning fumble with various bits of paper and an electronic pen on the end of a piece of string. The till bleeped half a dozen times and the computerized display unit regurgitated a new selection of green numbers which, I supposed, meant that the stock of refrigerators, double freezer types with room for odd bottles, had decreased by one. 'Monday, sir. It should arrive on Monday. D'you get a good congregation at your church?'

'Good, yes. Large, no.'

He emitted laughter so stylized that he might have been a parson himself. In a minute, we were out in the noisy street watching a shirt-sleeved policeman trying to put asunder two overheated motorists whose cars had joined unceremoniously together on the junction of Park Row and Greek Street. Barbara went to have something done to her hair and I decided to call on my old pal Ralph Jones, vicar of St Catherine's.

His parish was in South Leeds, in an industrial waste land between the railway and the canal. High rise flats grew out of the rubble as if all else had been bombed and they had miraculously escaped. Most of the old back-to-back houses had been pulled down but there were still a few shops, some boarded up, on the terrace that bordered the main road. The loud lorries threw up clouds of dust as they hurtled over what was left of the Highway Department's sand. There were cricket stumps chalked on the black churchyard wall and a few children were enjoying their own test match with the aid of a tennis ball, an old bat and a pile of coats. The church looked like Castle Dracula, Gothic revival at its most insane.

I thought I would peep inside before going to the vicarage round the back. There was a small door within the frame of the large door. It was like stepping into jail. But the interior was a vision of heaven: magnificent wood carvings in the choir and transepts; a stark but beautiful rood; and a reredos framed in gold and black, a glorious Madonna and Child. The smell of incense and brass polish. Cool and silent. A silence that seemed full of worship's echoes.

And there was Ralph, busying about the Lady Chapel with a yellow duster. He reminded me of the rapid salesman in the fridge shop.

'Peter!' He came round the altar and shook my hand vigorously, his voice resounding in that great space. Soon we were outside again in the heat and the glare.

'Which way are you taking me?'

'To the *new* vicarage!' He spoke the word *new* with a sort of sardonic triumph. 'Didn't I tell you they's finished it at last?' The old vicarage stood behind us, its windows boarded up, the grass in the front garden as long as that which nearly obscured the leaning gravestones. Ralph seemed to read my thoughts. 'Yes – and the windows in the new vicarage are boarded up as well. Quick work don't you think? I went for two days retreat at Mirfield and when I got back . . .' he made a swift gesture with his arms as if frightening birds.

'Who? Why?'

'*Why* must be left to the conjecture of social theorists. *Who* I can tell you: members of this parish, who else?'

'You must get sick and t——'

He raised a finger to cut short my remarks. 'Not all of 'em. They're not all like that, of course. But how many vandals does it take to smash eight window panes? Three, two . . .?' His voice trailed away.

We went into the vicarage which was clean, square and plain – like the waiting room in a suburban Health Centre. Ralph made some tea and we took it out into the back garden, which was quiet, screened from the narrow streets by a high wall.

'How long have you been here now, Ralph?'

'What is it, eight, nine years? I lose count.' He took a packet of cigarettes from his cassock pocket and rummaged around for matches.

'Are you looking for a move?'

'Not looking for a move, no. I like it here. It grows on you. Never a dull moment. I couldn't take your sleepy cows and everybody looking as if they'd fallen off an eighteenth-century water-colour.'

'Steady on! We're in the machine age as well, you know – what with tractors and motorbikes. And we've got vandals and graffiti.'

'Sorry, Peter. I didn't mean anything. I'm on edge. A bit harrassed you might say.'

'I'm not surprised. Look, Ralph, you've done your stint in the concrete jungle. Why don't you look for a change?'

He sat in silence for a minute, watching the ash accumulate on his cigarette. Then he stubbed it out violently in his saucer and stirred his tea in an absent-minded fashion.

'I said I'm not looking for a move, but I'm being moved all the same. Well, that's what it'll amount to. Grief! It makes me wonder who's running the Diocesan Office these days. First they build me a new vicarage – when I've told them I don't want one, anyway. Then they say they're going to have the church declared redundant.'

'Redundant?'

'You heard.'

'But why? It's not as if . . .'

'It's not as if we can afford to keep it going. That's the truth. They're not terrifically religious in South Leeds, Peter – not in the outward and visible sense, anyway. Not in the matter of coming to church every week and paying to keep a roof on the place!' He paused to drain his cup. 'Fact is, they can't afford to pay.'

'So?'

'So they'll board up St Catherine's like the vicarage windows. And the pastoral care of the people will be under the oversight – interesting word isn't it, "oversight" – of someone, it could be me, a mile and a half down the road at St John's.'

'That's not good.'

'That's putting it mildly!' He stood up quickly and poured the dregs of his tea over the lawn, with great care as if he was performing a religious ceremony. Another cigarette. I thought he looked pale, stark. A striking contrast between his black curly hair and his pasty face.

'Whereas, of course, what they need – the St Catherine's folk – is a man on the spot. They don't come to church so often, but they know me. I like to flatter myself they're even beginning to trust me. Look,' – he jabbed his cigarette in the direction of the nearest tower block – 'see that window at the end there? That's where Sharon lives. She's a young pro. Lives with her mum who's an old pro. Talk about private enterprise and family businesses! I was in court with them both yesterday. Some client turned out to be a nutter and tried to use Sharon's face as a dartboard. The next window. Well that's empty at the moment – the last tenant jammed the lock and just cleared off. Foul stinks – and when the Corporation blokes finally got around to breaking the door down, they found piles of rotting food and piles of . . . other stuff. Next one to that,' – he was like an eye patient, reading along a line of the optician's chart – 'there's an old lad lives by himself. He's just spent three months in the infirmary. Gangrene.'

It suddenly didn't seem to matter much whether our new fridge had one freezer compartment or two. I looked at the fraught, chain-smoking Ralph. 'And if you're on the spot, you can help them.'

'Well, there's not much you can do. Poverty and squalour has been the order of the day here for the best part of a hundred and fifty years. It'll take more than I can do to shift it. But you *know* it's a help just to be here. You can't go telling folk the church cares for them, then shift your office nearly two miles down the road.

'They know me, you see. They see me dodging about the place. And when I get my windows smashed in, well, they come and sympathize. Solidarity, you know. And what the Gas Board and the Water Board and the Electricity Board are to them, the Church of England's barmy bureaucracy is to me. So we swap tales of the most recent atrocities. Take that *human* contact away and what's left, eh?'

What could I say? I could hardly recount tales of rural hardship to measure against those of St Catherine's. I had begun that day more or less thoughtlessly, contemplating a trip into town that would be rather tedious, but looking forward to seeing Ralph, looking forward finally to getting back home to fresh air, peace and quiet, a pint in The Acorn. Now I felt enormously, immorally privileged – like the rich man who meets the blind beggar.

Ralph guessed my thoughts. 'There's no need to look like that, Peter. I know the countryside is no bed of roses, so to speak. You've got problems enough, I dare say. Old Canon Wilkinson once said to me, "You know Satan lodges in the towns, my boy; but he takes root in the country!" ' A thin smile across that too white face. Ash tumbling down the front of his cassock. 'But,' he pronounced the word like a man spitting, 'I haven't begun to tell you the worst. Do you know there are no plans at all for the preservation of St Catherine's interior, beyond putting it in the hands of the redundant churches people who will attend to emergencies and slap a brass plate on the door to tell folks their church isn't needed?

'I said, didn't I, that not many came to church? Twenty-five to the ten o'clock – we gave up Evensong last year. But it's still their church. Everybody's church, not just the ones who come, the committed and the zealous. And it's the only building in these parts that's at all beautiful. So we lock it up, call it "redundant", tell them they can only get in if they go to the proper authority for the key. That's deprivation, Peter, as sure as the lousy flats, the inadequate schools and all the rest. The secular authorities treat these people as casualties and problems, nuisances – instead of treating them like people who need decency, dignity and beauty. And now the Church is about to do the same. What can you do?'

What we did do was to go back inside the newly delapidated vicarage. From Ralph's study you could see the east wall of the old church and the huge stone carving of the apocalyptic angel with his trumpet. The doorbell rang and a posse of unkempt children arrived to ask if 'Father Jones wants any jobs'. An older child asked if they could be taken round the crypt again and shown the lead coffins. A fat man in a blue overall and a straw hat called to deliver fish. Ralph bought some kippers and shoved them in the fridge – and that reminded me I was due to meet Barbara.

'Come out and spend a day with us then,' I said, 'in Satan's countryside!' He grinned and said he would. Yet another fag as the church clock chimed five. He walked with me to the lychgate.

I met Barbara by the Civic Hall and by half-past six we were driving through the fields where the farmers were still at the harvesting. The place seemed bathed in colour, the air rich and clean. 'Tell me all Ralph's news,' said Barbara when the children were in bed and we were sitting out on the porch with iced drinks. I told her. She was very quiet for a minute or two, then she said, 'I went to St Catherine's when I was a girl. One of my friends was being confirmed there. It was the first place I'd seen the Sacrament reserved – and all that red and gold. It was like heaven to me. I hope they never close it down.'

That refrigerator arrived on Monday and insolently usurped the place of my old Bette-Davis-old-black-and-white-film-style-icebox. Ralph arrived three weeks later and told us that the authorities had now sold the land on which were the two vicarages, old and new. Ralph had moved into one of the flats nearby and a final decision on the future of St Catherine's had been postponed. He was keeping heaven open – for the time being.

13

THE FASTEST GUN IN THE VILLAGE

Kevin Murray was unimaginable without a gun in his hand. If it moved, Kevin shot it. Disconcerting to be opposite him at the bar in The Acorn and watch him screw up his left eye as he squinted at you over his pint: you felt he was taking aim. At the bar he stood in his stockinged feet – muddy boots left by the door – and still in his hat, telling us all an unlikely tale about 'natives' on some distant island who shot fish. 'It's less cruel, quicker – less mess. Cheaper as well. You only need a gun instead of all that expensive tackle.' He would have needed no persuading to start a roach shooting competition off Ouse Bridge in the middle of York.

Anyhow he was off to Scotland – or was it Wiltshire or the west coast of Ireland? – to shoot flesh, fish or fowl or any combination of all three. Location mattered nothing to Kevin. The only bit of territory he took any interest in was the distance between the end of his barrel and the moving target. He and Cleary the blacksmith were talking – which is to say that Kevin was talking and Michael Cleary was affecting a listening posture, his eyes glazed, his fingers fidgeting with his rapidly emptying pint glass.

Stan Fox came out of his smoky corner and clattered a number of pound coins on the bar. 'Same again please, landlord. One for Michael and a pint of gun oil for the twelve-bore bore here! Are you having one with me, Vicar?'

The jibe stung Kevin like a pellet.

'That's very Christian of you, Stan.'

'He's hankering after the vicar to give him a cut price funeral.' Kevin was squinting furiously out of that left eye. If he had had a gun in his hand, Stan Fox's obsequies would not have been long delayed.

Kevin didn't stay offended for long. You couldn't with Stan. He was so full of grinning good spirits, he could have insulted Her Majesty in front of the Royal Horseguards and got away with it.

'I don't reckon nowt to these one pound pieces. Wear out your pocket, they do.'

'Like shot,' said Kevin like lightning, contributing to his own caricature.

'I hear tell,' said Michael, 'there's a shoot on Saturday. Is that right, Kevin?'

Kevin stared mournfully into his glass. 'Aye it is right, Michael – more's the pity.'

Stan, astounded, said, 'More's the pity? Don't tell me the old dog's gone off his bones!'

Kevin missed the metaphor and began to make some reply to the effect that his hunting dogs were in good form. Realizing his mistake, he said, 'You heard me right. Shooting's not for me this weekend. There's a plan been hatched to take ladies with us. And guns and women don't mix – not in my books, they don't.'

'You never heard of Annie Oakley, Kev?'

'No, it's not that,' said Stan. 'He's scared the Missus'll take the opportunity to bump him off!'

Jokes were no laughing matter for poor Kevin. 'It's not that. It's just that shooting, well it's always been a man's game – traditional like – But if women are . . .'

'If women are going to spend the afternoon popping off dumb animals, who's going to get your dinner ready – that's about it, isn't it Kevin?' Molly, smoking one of her fancy coloured cigarettes and piping up from behind the bar. 'Just wait till I see your Jean. I'll tell her all about this male chauvinist piggery!'

'There'll be no need,' said Kevin, sadder than ever. 'It's all we've talked about for weeks. And tonight, just before I came out, we had an almighty bust up.'

'So you're drowning your sorrows, eh? Serves you right!' Gulping, Stan put his empty glass on the bar. 'Here, you can drown mine an' all. Same again, Molly!'

'Birds,' said Kevin. It might have been a swear word, to judge by the look on Molly's face.

'What are you calling us now, Mr Murray?'

He looked resigned. He spoke on a monotone. 'Nothing at all. You said "popping off dumb animals". Well we're not. And they aren't. It's a pheasant shoot.'

Molly utterly disregarded the confusion. 'Lovely things they are, too. I like to see them in the fields by the roadside. They ought to be ashamed of themselves, murdering God's creatures – didn't they, Vicar?'

I knew I was in the firing line. A discreet sip of my glass was the best part of theological valour. In the event I was rescued by Michael. 'Don't go dragging religion into sport. Some vicars shoots and some doesn't. Vicar of Barton now – he hangs pheasants in the church boiler house. Swears by it, so I'm told.'

Gun-toting wives, swearing vicars – it was time I went home!

It was late October, the air still and humid, the sun blood red, low in the sky over Johnson's barns. Gardeners were out. The Mickleovers were having a barbecue on the lawn. I was waylaid for ten minutes by their hospitality – a party for young Jane, she was leaving home to train as a nurse in Bristol.

I walked on past the newsagents and the garage

until I came to the big house on the corner that belonged to the Murrays. Jean Murray stood still as a monument in the upstairs window, clutching one of her husband's guns and pointing it right at me! I must have seen too many westerns for, quite involuntarily, I raised my hands. ('Reach for the sky, Reverend! You're a-gonna meet the Great Sheriff in the sky a whole lot sooner than you reckoned on!')

'Shh!' she hissed. Then she let go with both barrels. I was glad to discover that being dead did not feel at all bad. Jean Murray screamed: triumph, relief and panic all mixed. She dropped the gun and ran downstairs and out into the garden. 'I got him! I got him!' she cried exultantly, just as I was thinking gratefully, 'She missed me!' Then I saw it: sprawled out, grey, still, lifeless. It was the biggest, ugliest rat I had ever seen. Jean had recovered her composure. In a very matter of fact way she said: 'Kevin can dispose of that thing when he gets in from the pub. To think he says I couldn't hit a barn at ten paces!'

I stood at the gate for a few minutes then turned for the vicarage. Saturday morning saw Kevin and Jean off together in the Landrover to join the shoot.

Nowadays in The Acorn he has another line to shoot. How the Missus almost shot the Vicar and bagged herself a rat. It's the best tale of the lot!

14

PARISH FALLOUT

The Reverend Stephen Kershaw was vicar of St Martin's, Noston Gate with St Jude, Cline. Which is to say that he was village parson to the cluster of ageless lowlanders who lived in the changeless rustic quadrangle bordered by the church, two pubs and the war memorial. He was never quite sure what he was to the commuters in the Legoland super-homes which the private developers had tacked onto the edge of his parish like a swish new tail on a dour old dog.

At evening service on the Fourteenth Sunday after Trinity, there were exactly twelve people in his congregation when he announced that the Wednesday meeting of the Women's Institute in the Old Hall would be open to everyone because Miss Cynthia Tollance was coming to speak about Civil Defence – 'a matter which,' he addressed the twelve with apostolic urgency, 'must surely concern us all.' He had even put up a notice about it on the new estate.

At five minutes past eight on the following Wednesday, there were twenty-eight people spread out like a half-completed chess game over the neat rows of chairs which Jim Hardcastle, churchwarden, had carefully arranged in the Old Hall. This meant that some chairs were empty except for the bright red Civil Defence leaflet which the punctual Miss Tollance had efficiently distributed.

The fast fading light of the September sun cast dusty beams into the distant corners of the Old Hall and cloaked with a misty yellow haze the billiard table and the piano used (or as Mrs Whitehead of the WI whose job it was to play 'Jerusalem' at their every meeting liked to say, '*abused*') by the Sunday School. There were many who, if asked, would reply that Mary Whitehead was a powerful deterrent all by herself. At the far end of the room, below the old door which had lost the 'e' of its exit sign, were the various soft toys, slides and sand buckets which belonged to the newly formed playgroup. Mary Whitehead, wading through these bits and pieces, cried out in a loud voice, 'Not just Sunday School now, eh? But young 'uns are muckin' place up every day of week!'

The vicar smiled. Introducing Miss Tollance, he said that she needed no introduction. 'She looks as if she needs a good dinner,' said Jack Wilshaw as Miss Tollance took the stage. She was indeed thin, angular, wiry. She stood to attention for the whole of her speech: three-quarters of an hour of grey-haired moral conviction in tweeds. Then she sat down. The sun had set and the old Hall was as dark as a disused barracks. Hardcastle rumbled out of his seat and put the lights on. Two ladies of the WI nodded at each other like spies before making their way noiselessly to the kitchen. There would soon be a flicker of gaslight under the tea urn and Kershaw was silently grateful for it. He said he was sure that Miss Tollance had opened our eyes and given us much food for thought – Hardcastle muttered, 'It was me what put the lights on' – and he added something to the effect that nobody had had anything to eat yet.

It was time for questions. Arthur Greasby, a big man in those parts, whose family had farmed there since Cromwell's days, stood up and said tersely, 'Beggin' your pardon, ma'am but like as I'm only a farmer and not used to yer redemptive strikes . . .'

'Pre-emptive,' pre-empted Miss Tollance civilly, defensively.

Arthur continued unabashed, '. . . and yer megadeaths. But I would a' thought that, what wi' us bein' out i' t' country like, we wun't be needin' no special defence. We nivver 'ad nowt i' t'last set-to – 'cept keepin' t' blackout.'

Cups of tea and home-made cakes were being passed round as Miss Tollance, smiling, leapt to her feet to put Mr Greasby right. 'Ah! As I tried to explain, in the next war – which as I said will not be a conventional war (though, of course, it may *start* as a conventional war) – no one will be automatically safe just because he or she lives at a distance from the main centres of population.'

Greasby's neighbour, Mrs Johnson from the Old Manor, said she would get under the stairs as soon as the atom bombs started flying about – just as she did when there was a thunderstorm. In a louder tone she added, 'We have an outhouse made of very strong brick.'

Miss Tollance smiled, disarmingly, and said that not even the strongest brick . . . etc. She also thanked Mrs Wormald who had just given her some tea in a nice china cup. The vicar passed her a large piece of Doris Burton's chocolate cake.

There followed a good deal of fond reminiscence about the old Land Army in the last war, about the ME109 that had crashed on Stan Kipling's chicken run and about the handsome POW's who had been held in the vicinity. 'Such a polite man. He used to hold the door open for me when I took the officers' orders into the compound. You'd never have thought he was a *German*!' So said Mrs Lacey, still in her hat and poking her tongue into an eclair. All this talk was accompanied by generous chuckles – so many in fact, that Mrs Wearsdale was moved to suggest that the pleasant jocular mood had gone too far. Julia Wearsdale had only six months ago moved into the vicarage when the Church Commissioners had sold it in line with current policy and rehoused the vicar in a modern bungalow which bore the sign 'The New Vicarage'.

'In these anxious times,' said Mrs Wearsdale, eyeing the relaxed villagers who were well into their third cup of tea and fourth round of nostalgia, 'we must be properly protected. And I think the church crypt is the ideal place for it!'

There had been no four-minute warning given of that particular bombshell and the room at once fell silent as the crypt itself. Before anyone had a chance to say anything, she went on, 'And I should like to know what Miss Tollance makes of the idea.' 'And I'd like to know what Vicar meks on t'idea!' said Jim Hardcastle from under a cloud of smoke.

The vicar, who had been having quiet exploratory talks with Mrs Askham about the possibility of holding the garden fête in her grounds next year, was momentarily nonplussed. Miss Tollance, on the other hand, was ready with expert advice: 'How splendid! The crypt – below ground level of course – would be an excellent place for a shelter. It could almost certainly be equipped to provide a refuge for the whole village.'

There followed the most unruly WI meeting since that day in 1963 when they had fallen out over amendments to the rules about permitted methods of baking bread entered in the annual Noston Gate with Cline Show. Miss Tollance was suitably thanked by some and unthankfully glared at by others. Mrs Wearsdale was immediately shunned by half the gathering as the other half formed a coterie of her most sudden and devoted admirers. Mrs Whitehead tried in vain to launch a pre-emptive strike on the senile piano's silent middle D so that 'Jerusalem' could be more or less begun before it was more or less ended.

The next Thursday, the church was full as the vicar nervously introduced the Special General Meeting called hastily on the night of Mrs Wearsdale's putsch. James Standover, accountant and Treasurer of the Parochial Church Council, wondered how much it would all cost. The PTA said they would arrange a wine and cheese party to raise money. 'Holocaust permitting!' chortled one of the old villagers. Jim Hardcastle, who was the local joiner as well as churchwarden, asked how long it had been since anyone had ventured 'down there'. He said, 'There's beams down there as wouldn't support a swallow's nesting box, nivver mind your nooclear shelter.' Mrs Hetty

Raven thought the whole business ill-conceived, since it was sacrilegeous to use the church for secular purposes. This produced a fine debate which was, at times, almost mediaeval in its rural casuistry. When the vicar was asked for a ruling he said, 'In times past, churches have been used as places of sanctuary. So I can see nothing against the idea.' He was careful to add the words '– in principle.'

A campaigning unilateralist group from the Youth Club said it would all be a waste of time because there was no such thing as protection against nuclear weapons. The rest of the meeting, excited as they were by the ingenious novelty of the idea and its opportunities for subterranean romance, thought the Youth Club's view represented something of a damper and showed a lack of faith which some had regretfully come to expect from the young people of today. That caused an argument which was anything but casuistical and which was stopped only when Mr Standover again raised the question of cost. No one knew what to say until a business-like voice from about eight rows back on the pulpit side piped up, 'If the vicar, the wardens and the PCC are willing, I am prepared to do a preliminary feasibility study and could let the vicar have my findings in about ten days.' One of the Youth

Club mumbled loudly, 'If you can get the Russkies and the Yanks to hold their fire till then!'

'Who's 'e?' asked John Newbould of Jim Hardcastle. He was referring to the man in the pinstripes who had offered the feasibility study.

'I'll tell you who 'e is,' said Hardcastle in a voice that was neither as reverential nor as subdued as it ought to have been, given the holy surroundings. ''E's Simon Reddy, lives on t'new estate i' one o' them little boxes. Some sort o' tycoon or summat wi' Water Board. Likes sound on 'is own voice. T'ear 'im talk you'd reckon 'e were from t'Gas Board!'

But the feasibility study carried the day, or rather the night. It was past ten o'clock when the vicar put out all the lights and strolled across to the New Vicarage, weighing architectural modishness against those words from the Government's warning pamphlet: 'In the event of a nuclear explosion, bungalows afford scant protection.' It needed two cups of cocoa to settle his nerves after the unaccustomed excitement in his parish.

At nine o'clock next morning, his phone rang just as he was attacking his second rasher of bacon. 'Morning, Vicar,' said an urgent, high-pitched voice. 'It's Ron Blezzard from the *News*.'

'Bless Blezzard!' thought the Reverend Kershaw as he prepared himself for the explosion.

'Is it true, Vicar, that you've decided to turn your church into a nuclear fallout shelter?'

'What? No. It certainly is *not* true!'

'It's just that I got a firm line you were considering that very thing.'

The vicar thought uncharitable thoughts about putting a firm line round Ron Blezzard's neck. 'The *crypt*, Mr Blezzard. The crypt. And we're only at the discussion stage. Someone is doing . . . a feasibility study. Then we shall have to look closely at all the possibilities.'

'You're probably the first, you know.'

'What's that?' The vicar popped his plate back under the grill.

'The first parson in the country to turn your church into a nuclear shelter. Very original. Clever idea, Mr Kershaw!' It was like the Temptations in the Wilderness and with Blezzard as the flattering devil himself.

'Get thee behind me, Satan!' was Kershaw's thought as he repeated, 'I've told you once, it's not the church. Only, possibly, just possibly, the *crypt*.'

'But you'll keep me posted of any developments? Perhaps I could come out and see you?' Blezzard was a tenacious devil.

'Really there are no developments as yet. It would be wasting your time to come out and see me until the churchwardens and the PCC are able to be more definite.'

There was a ring of finality to the vicar's words. Even the devil is no match for bureaucracy and committees. Kershaw returned to his breakfast which had been rendered crispier by the radiant heat.

It was all there in the evening paper, cleverly put in the guise of a question next to a large picture of the church: 'Noston Gate to go Nuclear?' There was a picture of the vicar as well, copied from the one taken at his induction three years before. So poor Kershaw was not much surprised when the phone rang again that day and a friendly enough voice said, 'Hello Stephen. Archdeacon here. I wonder if I could call in for a cup of tea tomorrow afternoon? There are one or two things . . .'

Well, there were one or two things. Principally, one thing: 'What's all this hokum about turning the parish church into a nuclear shelter?'

At last everything was explained, including how necessary permission was, even more necessary in exceptional cases like this one. But the chain-smoking archdeacon said he knew Kershaw was a sound, sensible sort of chap who wouldn't 'do anything that would cause . . . difficulty'.

With this friendly archidiaconal warning tintinabulating in his ears and lighting his nightmares for more than a week to come, Kershaw tried to take refuge in the prosaic minutiae of wedding returns and the renewal of the Electoral Roll as he waited to see what the feasibility study might bring forth. Other refuge had he none, from the relentless barrage of phone calls from enquirers who wanted to know if it was all true, as one put it, '. . . that the government plans to use the churches as bomb-proof nuclear shelters in the event –' Kershaw cut him off. He began to wish the shelter were built already so that he could retreat to it and escape the phone.

The day before Mr Feasibility Reddy's report was due, the vicar answered an impatient ringer of his doorbell. It was a determined looking Julia Wearsdale from the Old Vicarage. 'Can I come in a minute, Mr Kershaw? It *is* rather important.'

They sat in the study: she under the window, he at his desk, twiddling his pen anxiously. 'Before Mr Reddy's report comes out, Vicar, I want to speak my mind: I am convinced we as a church have an absolutely overriding moral duty to provide that shelter for the parish. We have the space. There would be no excuse for us if we failed. No excuse for anyone who was given such a wonderfully clear opportunity to provide a service for his fellow man.'

Tired, overwrought, Kershaw said he noted her opinion – along with those of many others, not all of whom were in agreement. She should make her feelings plain to everyone at the meeting called to consider Mr Reddy's report.

Make them plain she did, before Reddy had risen to speak. 'I want this meeting to understand that we have a clear Christian duty to provide this shelter. And if Mr Reddy's report is adverse, we should get a second opinion.'

Sharon Norris announced that the PTA's cheese and wine party had raised £86 for the shelter fund. 'But there is no such fund yet, Mrs Norris,' said Kershaw, his mind tortured by images of Blezzard and the archdeacon. He wished the ground would open up and swallow him.

Jim Hardcastle remarked acidly, 'There's more folks 'ere who 'as an interest i' goin' under t'church as ivver came to fill t'pews!' Mrs Bowker thought committed church members should have priority when it came to allocating places in the shelter. 'Fire insurance for them who's bin born again,' whispered the Youth Club leader behind his hand.

At last Reddy was ready. He introduced his subject briskly and efficiently. 'Ladies and gentlemen, preliminary investigations have revealed that the crypt would not be a suitable place for a shelter. It is below the water table, and to concrete the whole area against wet would be prohibitive. In fact, it would be safer and cheaper to begin on a different site.'

Relief and annoyance spread across the faces in the company in about equal measure. Julia Wearsdale cried out, furiously, 'Shame!'

'However,' continued Reddy, 'when the men were down there, they discovered a disused passage, partly blocked, which leads up the slope to a cavernous underground area beneath the Old Vicarage. And the signs are that this is above the water level. But I offer this information incidentally. It's not really what we're here to discuss. It's not my brief to embarrass Mrs Wearsdale.' And he sat down.

Whether it was his brief or no, she was embarrassed all right. The vicar, beaming with relief, dismissed the meeting with a prayer after accepting Sharon Norris' kind proffering of the £86 to church funds.

Mrs Wearsdale left the building before the words of the Grace had died on the vicar's lips.

15

THE MEDIUM AND THE MESSAGE

I was with Bob Newburton, vicar of Carrow Dale, watching Yorkshire play Lancashire at Headingley. Even in the open air you couldn't avoid the whiff of Bob's cigars. It had been a cold, damp spring and the outfield was bright green. The sky was all liquid movement, yellow and blue; the watery sun sending black shadows racing across the ground.

'There's not many in for a Bank Holiday Monday,' said Bob.

'Weather's keeping 'em away I expect.'

'No,' he said loudly, almost with disgust. 'We used to watch cricket in all weathers. I was once at Bradford Park Avenue, when it snowed at Whitsuntide. No, it's all the sport they put on telly these days: folks won't leave their armchairs.'

Yorkshire were batting – badly. Thirty-nine for two. At last the big left-hander, newly promoted from the Colts, middled one and the crack echoed like a pistol shot round the under-populated arena. We had cans of ale in our hamper, but really it was hot tea weather.

'That's what we could do with,' said Bob.

'What, more tea?' I asked handing him the flask.

'Getting on the telly. The Church I mean.'

'Well, there's *Songs of Praise*, and usually a service on Sunday morning.'

'That's just the trouble: services on the box when folk ought to be in the pews. No, I mean we should be represented on prime time viewing. In the evenings, midweek, following the soap opera.'

'There's always the Epilogue.'

He scowled as he chewed the end of another cigar. 'Too late. Everybody's fallen asleep by the time the Epilogue comes on. Still, it's better than nothing I suppose.'

'How d'you reckon they decide which parsons they're going to let do epilogues?'

'Well, it's all a – good shot, Geoff! Fifty up at last! Not before time! – it's all a matter of who you know. Friends of the producer. Folks like that who've got themselves well in.'

'I wish Yorkshire would get themselves well in!'

That night, waking from a doze through the holiday horror film, I thought again about what Bob had said. I hit on this wild idea to test his hypothesis. Was it really only folks who were well in who were allowed to present epilogues? Just then the Epilogue came on: a nice old parson with a red face and a twinkle in his eye, reminding us that 'holiday' comes from 'holy day'. I looked hard for signs of well-in-ness, but he just looked like an ordinary parson to me. I decided then and there that I would write a few scripts and send them in. It took me about a fortnight to write four. Sermons jazzed up a bit – that's how I thought of them.

Six weeks later, I was in the bath when Barbara came in with a big brown envelope. 'It's the television people – they've sent your scripts back.' The news poured cold water over my ego even as Barbara poured warm water over my back. That was that then. Perhaps it was a case of being well in after all. Or maybe the scripts just weren't much good. Later, I looked at the letter which came with the rejected work.

Dear Mr Mullen

Thank you for letting us see your scripts for the Epilogue which we have read with interest. The Producer, Richard Whaley, is of the opinion that they might make a series – if you are prepared to make a small number of alterations and a few stylistic changes. For example, such phrases as 'Inherently and ineluctably wicked' represent purple passages, rather. You could say simply 'truly wicked'. And remember that these scripts are supposed to be *talks*, not essays: so 'It is' should become 'It's', 'they are' 'they're' and so on.

If you are willing to make these adjustments, we will send you the necessary pro-forma that we send to all our Epilogeans together with a date and time for you to come to the studio for a recording session.

All good wishes

Yours sincerely

Lorna Travis-Page

So I was to be an Epilogean! How exciting it was to repeat silently to myself words like 'studio' and 'recording session' and, of course, 'necessary pro-forma'. I was ribbed about it mercilessly by the family: 'If they put you on after the horror film, people will think it's the horror film part three!' Barbara wanted to know what I was going to wear. 'Your clerical shirts are getting really tatty.' So I got a couple of new shirts out of the adventure.

The 'necessary pro-forma' arrived one Friday morning. Actually, it contained firm instructions about what to wear: not white things because these can become 'see-through' under the studio lights; not dazzly shirts and ties. Pastel shades were best. A dog collar was all right. They wanted to know what I was going to call my series. (I had written four talks on different sorts of love.) I thought of 'Ways of Loving', but Barbara said people might stay up expecting sex education and they would be disappointed when they got me instead. She said, 'Call it "All You Need is Love", then you can use the Beatles song as your theme music.' So that is what I wrote down on the 'necessary pro-forma'.

When the day dawned, I was all for backing out. It had been a flight of fancy, a presumption. I would telephone my apologies and leave the job to those who were well in. But no; I overcame my nerves sufficiently to drive to the studio, walk through the revolving doors and introduce myself to the receptionist who sat beneath gigantic still shots of all our favourite stars. She said she would call Mr Whaley for me. Would I take a seat? So I sat among the tall rubber plants and between the two aquaria full of tropical fish. There was a thick brown carpet. Three or four monitors high on the wall broadcast the station's programmes. In a couple of minutes a delightful young lady, with a flashing smile and a clipboard, arrived and introduced herself: 'I'm Sally Emmet-Barnes, a researcher attached to the Epilogue.' Lorna Travis-Page, Sally Emmet-Barnes: how strange! I did not yet know that all researchers and assistants in television are called something like Sara Doublebarrel; all dress in stylish ethnic clothes and nod respectfully towards the glossier images of feminism; all seem to have just had a year off to give birth to a baby who is usually called Titania or Reuben. They are all very nice, helpful ladies, who make allowances for the unwithitness of bumbling amateur Epilogeans who are not yet well in.

I followed her short skirt and jingling gold belt up the narrow staircase and through the endless series of fire doors that led to Mr Whaley's office. Richard Whaley was a tall man whose clothes nevertheless seemed a little too big for him. He had a sparse white beard and he smoked cigars that smelt more expensive than those of the vicar of Carrow Dale.

'Well then, Peter, let's go to the studio.'

The studio was full of people who seemed to be attached to various gadgets, waiting for something to do. A man perspiring in shirt sleeves called out, 'Dick, is it set up and call time at O eleven twenty, and d'you want the clock before light up?' It was a lingo more obscure than New Testament Greek. We passed through the studio to make-up, where another young woman put powder on my face. It was like a hall of mirrors with the aroma of a ladies' hairdressers. She asked me how I usually wore my hair. I told her it was wearing thinner.

Back in the studio, it was boiling under the

lights. I imagined I was in an operating theatre. I suppose people had got into the habit of whispering, but to me it seemed unnaturally quiet. There was a huge free-standing board with a caption chart that said 'The Epilogue', and a picture of the street scene which I had chosen to go with the Beatles song. I was in the famous chair at last! A glass of water on the low table beside me. A few musty books to provide the atmosphere of a parson's study. But the backdrop was light blue cardboard.

I could hardly make out the face of the director as he gave me instructions from somewhere out in a black void behind the blazing lamps. The make-up girl came out to dab my nose end. Then the director asked me to give him a voice level: 'Just tell us what you had for breakfast, Peter.' I couldn't remember. 'That's fine!' he said, and we began a short rehearsal. It was an experience to see my hand-written scripts turned into glorious print and transferred to the autocue.

When we were getting ready, Richard had told me a story about an old parson who used to come and do epilogues before the days of autocue.

'This chap was the best storyteller I've ever heard,' he said. 'I told him simply to keep on talking until one of our men, off camera, would give him a signal that there were thirty seconds left. All very discreet of course, and beyond the viewer's line of vision. This old boy said he understood. But he was so nice, so courteous, that when our man gave the signal, he leaned forward gracefully and in full view of our audience of about two million, interrupted his story to say, "Thank you so much!" ' Richard chortled. I smiled. The make-up girl came out to dab me again. And then we were recording.

I was astonished to see that, amid all the ultra-modern equipment of the television studios, they still use the old wooden clapper-board with the number of the programme and the 'take' written on it in chalk. My own voice burbling along for four four-minute spells and surrounded by absolute silence was an odd, lonely experience. I had little rushes of panic when I thought I couldn't go on, but eventually I reached the bottom line of the autocue and the silence was broken reassuringly by the Beatles and 'All You Need is Love'.

I was fast learning a new language about 'audio sets', 'caption inserts' and 'going clear' – this last expression meant sitting still until the technicians checked that the programmes had actually recorded. Luckily they had: I could not have gone through the process again, even if they had given me star billing.

Miss Emmet-Barnes reappeared, the gold belt

jingling as she wiggled across the studio. 'There, that's done with,' she said, as if she had just nursed me through a painful exploratory operation. She carried a small key on a huge wooden key ring. 'I'll take you to a dressing room and you can wash off your make-up.' Back we went down the labyrinthine corridors and through the innumerable fire doors until I reached a small cubicle that was all narrow mirrors and pink soap. 'There, I'll leave you to freshen up. Mr Whaley will be along when he's finished downtracking.' Now 'freshen up' I could understand; it went with 'automobile', 'sidewalk' and 'take a raincheck' – the argot of the international media. But 'downtracking' was another of those technical phrases which helped obscure the workings of that media from all but the initiated.

Richard Whaley appeared, smiling, just as I was enjoying fiddling with the sink top switch that dimmed the light over the mirror. It was the same pink light as that in Father Christmas's Grotto at Lewis's department store. Whaley added to the seasonal flavour with a whiff of his cigar. 'Come on, old chap, and we'll have some lunch!' 'Old chap!' Perhaps I was on the way to becoming 'well in'!

Lunch was served by swift waitresses who wore the name of the television company printed on their aprons. I ordered a ham salad. Even the packets of mustard and salad cream came bearing the station's monogram.

'How long have you worked for television, Richard?'

He looked and talked as if he had been born to the trade. But he said, 'Only about five years. At one time, I was intending to go into your business.'

'The Church of England?'

'Well no – not exactly.' And he added quietly, as if naming a rival television company, 'Methodist, actually.'

'But you didn't go through with it?'

'I didn't become a minister, if that's what you mean. But I reckon our jobs are similar, don't you? We've both got to get up front and communicate. We're both in the presentation business.'

I supposed we were.

'Will you,' he asked over the jam roly-poly, 'come back and do some more epilogues?'

It was very nice to be asked. I said I would try to screw up the courage. He smiled again and the little white beard seemed to spread all over his chin. He said, 'Give me a TV camera and an autocue and I'll talk all day. But don't ask me to do what you do – stand up in an empty pulpit and talk. I'd rather run a mile.'

They see you off the premises in television

studios. This is always done very precisely – it was the only formal part of my visit – as a security precaution following some of the terrorists' threats of the 1970's. Sally Emmet-Barnes saw me off, too. She had this habit of calling me 'Reverent'. 'See you next time then Reverent. Cheers!'

Three weeks later the epilogues came on television. As I gazed bleary-eyed – they were broadcast at 12.15 am – at my image on the screen, all the glamour, unreality and panic of my recording session came rushing back. The family giggled and made jokes about megastars in dog collars.

Those epilogues, though not exactly the sort of evangelistic miracle the vicar of Carrow Dale had imagined that day at the cricket ground, were watched by many of my parishioners. And I always thought country folks went to bed early! Mrs Barlow, who helps out at the post office, called on her way home from work. She is, to put it kindly, a rather infrequent churchgoer. 'You were on the telly, Vicar,' she said, as if this were the first I had heard of it. 'We watched you every night. We did think you were good. When shall we be seeing you again?'

I knew the answer to that one: 'Well, how about Parish Communion in St Luke's at 9.45 on Sunday?'

16

A BIT OF FIRE

Michael Duffield is the best organist in the world. But then, every vicar who has a reliable, conscientious bloke in charge of the pipes and stops knows he has the best organist in the world. And by the word 'bloke' I mean to include Amy Redfern in her blue three-cornered hat and steel-rimmed glasses down at St Chad's.

'What about the Harvest, Vicar?' asked Duffield one Sunday as he was stowing away the anthem sheets after Evensong.

'The usual, I think.' It was the safest reply to an organist. All organists hate change. Moreover, they can detect any hint of change at thirty leagues. It all comes out of the same sensitivity that makes them into such admirable musicians, I suppose; but it can be testing to have to grapple constantly with their finely tuned antennae, to be always on guard against seeming to say the wrong thing. So 'the usual' was an automatic reply.

Imagine my flabbergastedness then, when Duffield said, 'Well, I was hoping we might do something a bit different.' He bent to pick up a fallen copy of Walford Davies and his surplice caught on a nail. 'Dash it!' he said (or words to that effect). 'It's time I got myself a new cassock as well.' The one he wore was faded blue and threadbare sure enough, but new cassocks and the idea of some new music for Harvest, was too much for me to take in in one go. I answered with one of Duffield's favourite questions: 'What's wrong with the way we did it last year?'

He sat down on an old chest that was full of music he had been meaning to clear out. 'Nothing's *wrong* with what we've always done, but I reckon we need something with a bit more fire.'

Fire at Harvest means burning stubble in these parts. He took a delapidated comb to his long grey fringe. 'You see, the way I look at it, Vicar – every year we have "We Plough the Fields and Scatter", and . . .' (he began one of his legendary digressions) '. . . they can't sing it right. "We plough the fields and scatter," they sing, as if they meant "We do the work and buzz off". Congregations always take their breaths at the wrong time . . .' (Duffield by contrast hardly paused for breath at all.) '. . . and "Come Ye Thankful" – and they're not thankful at all. And "To Thee O Lord Our Hearts We Raise". Aye, we sang that last year as well, after that long-winded preacher you went and got for us.

We should have been raising glasses not hearts by the time he finished.'

'Well, what d'you suggest, Michael?'

He became calmer when he realized there was no immediate opposition to his plans. 'I've one or two ideas. Nothing definite yet. But, as I said, a bit more fire.'

'"Come ye thankful people" has quite enough fire in it for me.' I repeated the lines

And thine angels charge at last
In the fire the tares to cast.

'Aye, well,' said Duffield, 'we know where we can get summat to quench fire.'

A couple of pints in The Acorn fuelled his expansiveness and he told me just what he had in mind to put fire into St Luke's harvest.

'The usual Harvest hymns – they're not really about the fruits of the earth: most of 'em are nasty little verses about ordinary folks being sent to hell – like in the lines you quoted back in the vestry. What we want are some real hymns that rejoice in the good earth.'

'There are always the Psalms.'

'Aye, and folks can't sing 'em! Your average man in the pew knows *The Parish Psalter* about as well as he knows the Hong Kong telephone directory.'

'Who's off to the mystic east, then?' Jack Ellis looked up from his large scotch and his mucky tales. He offered cigarettes from a flashy case engraved with his initials.

'I've spent enough time out there,' said Duffield, refusing the cigarette and fumbling for his pipe. And I had to wait for further news of how he planned to add fire to the harvest while he added some to his briar and while he embarked on another legendary digression, this time about the pros and cons of the Far East. (Yes, now I reflect, those words are an accurate description of what Duffield found in Bangkok!) At length, Jack Ellis ran out of smutty stories and, giving the reason that he was off to watch his video of Fellini's 8½, left the pub.

'Folk songs,' said Duffield. 'I've found a volume of old songs about farming and feasting. What if we were to start the service with one of the so-called well known hymns, then sing a few of these songs? And we could have a few readings from the nature poets . . .'

'You mean, why don't we have a pagan Harvest?'

'No – well, yes. Not exactly. But something more genuinely of the earth – earthy, if you know what I mean. Make a change from all that moral blackmail – using harvest as a symbol of judgement every verse-end. It's not judgement, anyway; it's mercy, blessing. Any excuse the hot-gospellers get and they'll . . .'

'You don't like hot gospel, but you'd like to add fire eh?'

'Not hell-fire though. Something that's more to do with everyday reality.'

The little bar was quiet, the lights dim, the musak switched off, the landlord in his cubby hole doing his paperwork for the brewery. Duffield shouted, 'Jim, we're dying of thirst out here!' Jim Hargreaves emerged, a pencil in his teeth, a wad of computer printouts in his hands: 'Help y'self Michael, will you – seein' as there's only you and the Vicar. I'm snowed under just now.' The beer pumps were as familiar as organ pumps to Duffield.

Halfway down his third pint, he said conspiratorially, 'Some of those folk songs make nice little dance tunes too.' I nearly choked on my milk stout. Could this be the same Michael Duffield who had found the Gospel dancing team from the theological college so insufferable?*

I put it to him, 'Don't tell me you're a convert to dancing in the aisles, Michael!'

I agreed to attend the next choir practice where I would hear the down to earth songs. At twenty past ten we staggered off down the village street,

*See *Rural Rites*.

Duffield humming gaily what must have been one of the proposed tunes for the fiery harvest.

Well, they really did sound good. Rather like madrigals, the choir in four parts, the occasional round. Very English. Delightful. And they did not require organ accompaniment, so Michael was free to go in for a bit of discreet conducting. Evocative phrases and titles: 'In the Ninth Month of the Year'; 'Follow Fields and Fells' and Duffield's favourite, 'In Church and Inn'.

The PCC were not so easily convinced: 'Are we not having a proper Harvest then this year, Vicar? What's up wi' "We plough the fields and scatter?" ' asked Tom Sedgeman, bearing out the truth of Duffield's criticism of folks' reading of that hymn.

'I'd rather have Evensong as usual.'

'What about lessons – readings, like?'

It was what arose out of my answer to that question which finally persuaded most of them to fall in with my (i.e. Duffield's) scheme. I said, 'Well, I hope you'll all volunteer to come and read your favourite nature poetry.'

And they did. We had Nellie Webster in her midwife's outfit reading 'Season of mists and mellow fruitfulness'. John Swallow, the architect, who occasionally wrote highbrow book reviews for the national dailies, gave a dulcet reading of 'Glory be to God for dappled things'. We had some Wordsworth, two lots of Shelley and part of 'Little Gidding' – next to the head choirboy's offering of a remnant of Noel Coward. We ended with 'Come ye thankful people', and my eyes were beginning to move towards the tables laden for supper at the back of the church, when I smelt a funny smell. At the same time, something seemed to go wrong with the pitch of the organ. Like a record on an uneven turntable, it started to 'wow' and 'flutter'

Grant O Lord of Life that we
Holy grain and pure may be . . .

we sang, as a cloud of very impure smoke seeped out from above the organ manual. The choir began to cough. The smoke filled the nave and the congregation looked as if they were on the filmset of *Gaslight*.

And thine angels charge at last
In the fire the tares to cast . . .

we spluttered on. Tongues of flame shot out of the back vestry behind the organ. *Götterdämmerung!* The choirmen recoiled, but Duffield continued his playing like Captain Nemo himself at the keyboard of his blazing, sinking *Nautilus*.

Steve Merryweather (bass), Karen Dickinson

(contralto) and one of the wardens manhandled the fire extinguisher. They quickly doused the flames and normal service was resumed as soon as possible. There were many jokes over the Harvest Supper. Merryweather said, 'I reckon you were smoking your pipe, Michael, and dropped it in the bellows!' Nellie the midwife was very subdued as she asked, 'You don't suppose it could have been a bolt from the blue, do you, Vicar? You know, as a judgement on these . . . goings on?'

I said, 'A few misdirected volts from the Central Electricity Generating Board, if you ask me. Anyhow, Mr Duffield will tell you that Harvest is about mercy, not judgement – isn't it Michael?'

'Aye, a fuse,' was all he said.

As we took our ale later, I asked him, 'Well then, what are you going to suggest for Harvest next year, old man?'

He eyed his empty glass. 'Same as I'm suggesting now, Peter: same again!'

So we did. And the fire was quenched.